Chairs

Written by Mary-Anne Creasy
Photography by Michael Curtain

sundance™

This is my mom's chair.

This is my dad's chair.

This is my sister's chair.

This is my brother's chair.

This is my grandpa's chair

This is my cat's chair.

This is my chair.